D0535697

To Mel, who is not really smelly, and to the little
stinkers in her life.
— KLW

Published in 2014 by Simply Read Books | www.simplyreadbooks.com
Text © 2014 Kari-Lynn Winters
Illustrations © 2014 Paola Opal

Library and Archives Canada Cataloguing in Publication

Winters, Kari-Lynn, 1969-, author
Stinky skunk Mel / written by Kari-Lynn Winters ; with illustrations by
Paola Opal.

ISBN 978-1-897476-83-3

I. Opal, Paola, 1976-, illustrator II. Title.

PS8645.I5745S75 2013   jC813'.6   C2011-900534-4

We gratefully acknowledge for their financial support of our publishing program the
Canada Council for the Arts, the BC Arts Council, and the Government of Canada through the Canada
Book Fund (CBF).

Manufactured in Malaysia.

Book design by Paola Opal and Heather Lohnes.

10 9 8 7 6 5 4 3 2 1

KARI-LYNN WINTERS

STINKY SKUNK MEL

illustrated by PAOLA OPAL

SIMPLY READ BOOKS

When he raised his tail,

he sprayed a bad smell—

and everyone knew,

it was STINKY SKUNK MEL!

"STOP!" they cried.

"It smells worse than feet.

It's bad. It's rotten.

Like moldy old meat!"

Mel tried to listen.

He really did care.

But when he got nervous,

he SPRAYED in the air.

"I can't stop spraying
my STINKY skunk smell.
It's just who I am,"
said Stinky Skunk Mel.

So SMELLY young Mel
lost his friends in this way.
He couldn't stop spraying
that stinky skunk spray.

On the outskirts of town,

where no one would roam,

he found an OLD TIRE

to be his new home.

He curled up inside
that dirty old tire.
Then he wheezed, "Ah, ah, ah..."
and he sneezed, "Ah, ah, ah...CHOO."
He could smell FIRE!

SIRENS rang out
through the smoky, grey haze.
Fire trucks were coming
to put out the blaze.

Out jumped the fighters
with all of their gear.
Some led the way.
Some took the rear.
Fighting the fire
took teamwork and aim.
They FLOODED the stump
to put out the flame.

They poked at the roots,

inspected the bark,

and checked it once more

—when Mel saw a SPARK.

It bounced off a rock

(it was quite hard to see)

and started to burn

the forest debris.

"Oh no!" cried Mel,

his tail in the air.

The fighters turned back

to SOAK the new flare.

CRACK went the fire!
Oh, how it popped!
Then something happened...
the hose water stopped!

The others were nervous.

They ran far away.

Then Mel turned around and...

SPRAYED his skunk spray.

Oh, this ending

could have been tragic...

but the fire just fizzled

and went out like MAGIC.

They ran to young Mel
and held him up high.
Hooray for their hero!
Oh, what a guy!

"Hooray! Hooray!
For STINKY SKUNK MEL!
He may still stink.
But, hey, he's just swell!"

Then they all worked together
to fix the burnt stump,
so Mel could live there—
and not in the dump.

And when they had FIRES
and trouble with HOSES,
they gave MEL a call...

and pinched closed their noses.

about KARI-LYNN WINTERS

Kari-Lynn Winters is the author of *Runaway Alphabet* (Simply Read Books), *On My Walk* (Tradewind Books), *Jeffrey and Sloth* (Orca Book Publishers), and *Gift Days* (Fitzhenry and Whiteside). Besides being an award-winning children's author, Kari-Lynn is also an experienced playwright and theatre performer, a certified teacher, and an academic scholar. She lives in St. Catharines with her husband, two children, and four cats. For more information visit www.kariwinters.com.

about PAOLA OPAL

Paola Opal is illustrator and co-author of the Simply Small board book series and has recently helped develop one of the books into app format. Paola has been a graphic designer for over fifteen years and is a recipient of the Alcuin Society Award for Excellence in Book Design for *One Little Bug* (Simply Read Books), which she wrote and illustrated under the name Paola van Turennout. She currently lives in South Surrey, BC. For more information visit www.paolaopal.com.